A Note to Parents and Caregivers:

Read-it! Joke Books are for children who are moving ahead on the amazing road to reading. These fun books support the acquisition and extension of reading skills as well as a love of books.

Published by the same company that produces *Read-it!* Readers, these books introduce the question/answer pattern that helps children expand their thinking about language structure and book formats.

When sharing a book with your child, read in short stretches, pausing often to talk about the pictures and the meaning of the book. The question/answer format works well for this purpose and provides an opportunity to talk about the language and meaning of the jokes. Have your child turn the pages and point to the pictures and familiar words. Read the story in a natural voice; have fun creating the voices of characters or emphasizing some important words. And be sure to re-read favorite parts.

There is no right or wrong way to share books with children. Find time to read with your child and pass on the legacy of literacy.

Adria F. Klein, Ph.D.
Professor Emeritus
California State University
San Bernardino, California

Look for the other books in this series:
Animal Quack-Ups: Foolish and Funny Jokes About Animals (1-4048-0125-1)
Chewy Chuckles: Deliciously Funny Jokes About Food (1-4048-0124-3)
Dino Rib Ticklers: Hugely Funny Jokes About Dinosaurs (1-4048-0122-7)
Galactic Giggles: Far-Out and Funny Jokes About Outer Space (1-4048-0126-X)
School Buzz: Classy and Funny Jokes About School (1-4048-0121-9)

Editor: Nadia Higgins
Designer: John Moldstad
Page production: Picture Window Books
The illustrations in this book were prepared digitally.

Picture Window Books
5115 Excelsior Boulevard
Suite 232
Minneapolis, MN 55416
1-877-845-8392
www.picturewindowbooks.com

Printed in the United States of America.

Library of Congress Cataloging-in-Publication Data
Dahl, Michael.
Monster laughs : frightfully funny jokes about monsters /
written by Michael Dahl ; illustrated by Brandon Reibeling.
p. cm. — (Read-it! joke books)
Summary: An easy-to-read collection of jokes about vampires,
mummies, and other monsters.
ISBN 1-4048-0123-5 (library binding)
1. Monsters—Juvenile humor. 2. Wit and humor, Juvenile. [1.
Monsters—Humor. 2. Riddles. 3. Jokes.] I. Reibeling, Brandon, ill.
II. Title. III. Series.
PN6231.M665 D34 2003
818'.5402—dc21
                                                          2002156390

Monster
Laughs
Frightfully Funny Jokes About Monsters

Michael Dahl • Illustrated by Brandon Reibeling

Reading Advisers:
Adria F. Klein, Ph.D.
Professor Emeritus, California State University
San Bernardino, California

Susan Kesselring, M.A., Literacy Educator
Rosemount-Apple Valley-Eagan (Minnesota) School District

PICTURE WINDOW BOOKS
Minneapolis, Minnesota

Why don't monsters eat clowns?

They taste funny.

What kind of music do mummies like?

Wrap.

Why doesn't the vampire have many friends?

Because he's a pain
in the neck.

What does the cyclops eat for dessert?

Eyes cream.

What dogs are the best pets for vampires?

Bloodhounds.

What do you say to a two-headed monster?

"Hello, hello!"

What kind of jewelry do ghosts like to wear?

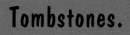

Tombstones.

What do you get when you cross a ghost with a firecracker?

Bamboo!

What should you do if you meet a blue monster?

Try to cheer it up!

What's a vampire's favorite sport?

Batminton.

What do you give King Kong when he sneezes?

Plenty of room!

What did the big, hairy monster do when he lost a hand?

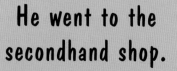

He went to the
secondhand shop.

Why couldn't the mummy answer the phone?

He was tied up.

Why was the ghost wearing a bandage?

It had a boo-boo.

Why wasn't there any food left after the monster party?

Because everyone was a goblin.

How can you
tell if there's
a monster
under your bed?

Your nose touches the ceiling.

What musical instrument did the skeleton play?

The trom-bone.